The
Blue
Elephant

Zoo Stories

The
Blue
Elephant

Kate Noble

Illustrations
Rachel Bass

Silver
Seahorse
Press

No part of this publication may be reproduced or transmitted in any
form or by any means, or stored in any information storage and
retrieval system without prior written permission of the publisher,
Silver Seahorse Press, 2568 North Clark Street,
Suite 320, Chicago, IL 60614
Distributed to the trade by Lifetime Books, Inc., Hollywood, FL 33020

ISBN 0-9631798-3-7

First Edition
Manufactured in the United States of America
1   2   3   4   5   6   7   8   9   10

Sassi wiggled her trunk at the children. They were waiting for her to do something larky, but she didn't feel larky. She was sad. She wanted

some water to play in. Sassi came

to the zoo from a park in Africa. She

loved the zoo. The children came to

see her every day. The food was good.

The keepers who took care of her were fun.

Most of all, Sassi loved Lina, the Indian elephant

who told wonderful stories.

What Sassi longed for

was a big muddy pond

like the wallow where she played

in Africa.

In a wallow, Sassi could get down in the water and roll

in the mud. She often told Lina how much fun wallows are.

When Lina saw that Sassi was sad, she said, "Don't worry, child. I have a plan to tell the keepers about the wallow. When you go on your morning walk, take them to water. How many places in the zoo have water?"

Sassi thought. "There's the Sea Lion Pool, but there's no mud there."

"Never mind the mud, child. The first step is water. Where else?"

"The Duck Pond. Plenty of mud in there. And there's the fountain in the garden."

"Good. Here's the plan."

Sassi listened. She could hardly wait for morning.

Bright and early Sassi set off on her walk

with the keepers. When they reached the path

to the Sea Lion Pool, she broke away and ran.

She lifted her head. She trumpeted loudly.

The sea lions jumped into the water and

swam in frantic circles. The keepers came running.

Sassi trumpeted again and pointed at the water.

"Sassi," the woman said sternly, "Stop that."

"Sassi," the man said sternly, "Stop that."

They weren't paying any attention to the water. She pointed at the water.

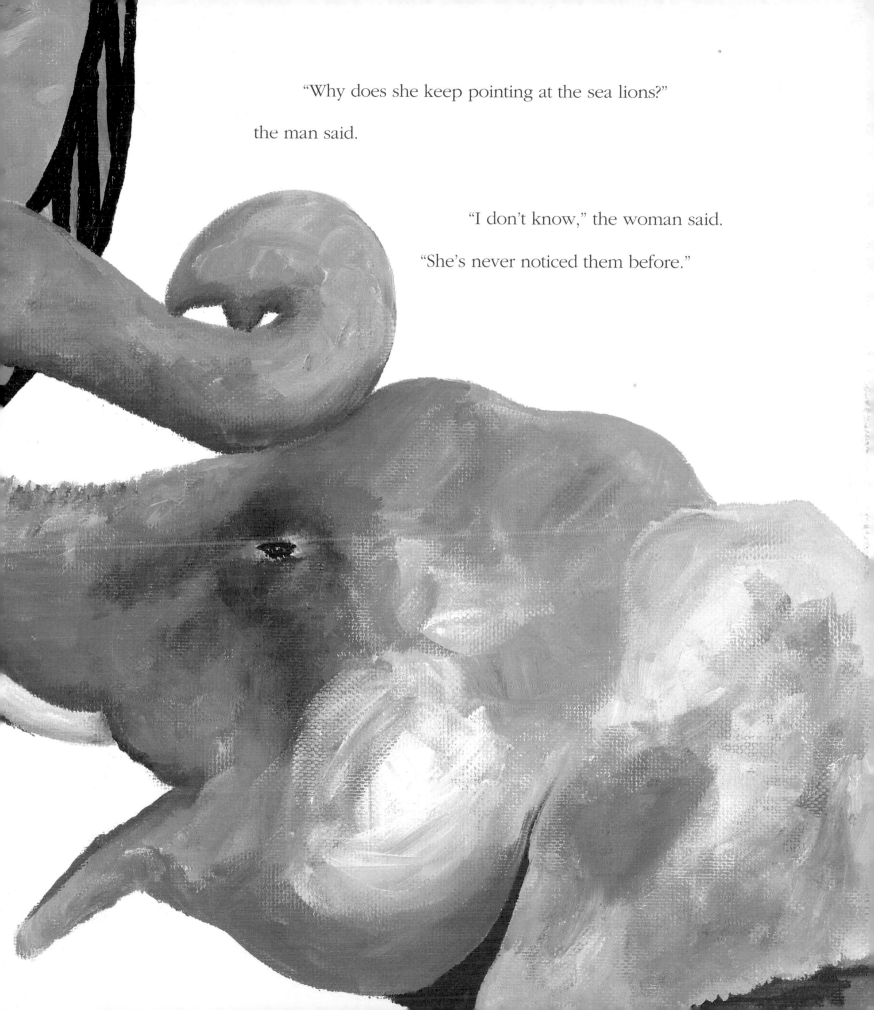

"Why does she keep pointing at the sea lions?"

the man said.

"I don't know," the woman said.

"She's never noticed them before."

When the keepers led her home, Lina was waiting.

"Well?"

"Nothing," Sassi said.

"Didn't you get away?"

"I got away. I trumpeted my head off. I pointed at the water. I did everything but dive in. They didn't notice."

"Child, how on earth could they not notice?"

"Oh, they noticed what I was doing. They just didn't understand."

"Well," Lina said, "this was only the first step. Tomorrow, you'll do the Duck Pond."

The next day when the keepers brought Lina

back, they closed the gate and left. Sassi was stunned.

Weren't they going to take her out?

"Lina," Sassi cried, "What happened?"

"We need a new plan."

"Why?"

"They talked about yesterday the whole time.

They think you're turning wild or some such foolish

thing. They're not going to take you out until next week."

"Turning wild?" Sassi was thrilled.

"We can try one more time," Lina said, "but the Duck Pond is out.

You put the sea lions in a tizzy that lasted for hours. There's no telling

what you'd do to those ducks. Try the fountain in the garden."

"They won't take me to the garden," Sassi said.

"No, they won't take you, but you're a lot bigger then they are.

Just go slowly. Don't trumpet this time. Just edge up to the water.

Point at it. Calmly."

"I'll try."

When the keepers finally took Sassi out again, they were almost back home before she saw the garden. The keepers had been tense at first. Now they were strolling along. Sassi ambled toward the side of the path. At the opening to the garden, she turned and moved slowly toward the fountain.

The woman pushed Sassi behind
the ear, trying to turn her. Sassi kept
going. The woman jumped in front of
her, and Sassi didn't know what to do.
Then she had an idea. It made her smile.

She reached down and lifted the woman with
her trunk. She carried her forward and gently set
her down in the fountain. The woman gasped. The
man laughed. Sassi wiggled her trunk at them.

"Sassi, you naughty girl," the woman said, but her voice didn't sound angry. Sassi dipped her trunk into the fountain and sprayed water on the man. Then she sprayed some on herself. Now maybe they would understand.

They sputtered and scolded
and then they all headed for home.

The woman said, "Why is Sassi
doing these funny things?"

The man laughed. "As elephants
go, she's still a kid. She's just playing."

Not one word about water.

Thunder boomed and lightning flickered across the sky.

Lina called, "Come inside."

"No," Sassi said.

"You'll get a chill."

"I don't care. If I get sick, they'll wish they had tried to understand." She lay down in a patch of dirt.

The rain came thick and fast. The dirt turned to mud. It was cold, but the mud was so lovely that Sassi rolled in it. She splashed. She raised her head and trumpeted into the storm. She hadn't had so much fun since she was a tiny little elephant.

The keepers watched her.

"Look at her playing in the mud,"
the woman said. "That's what she
wants. Water. Don't you see. It's the
mud and the water."

The man stared. "You're right.
She took us to water to tell us. She
wants a wallow like they make for
elephants in Africa."

Sassi stood up. She nodded her head. Then
she wiggled her trunk. The keepers laughed.

"Okay Sassi," the man said, "we'll get you
a wallow. We promise."

Sassi tilted her head back and trumpeted
again. She couldn't wait to tell Lina.

—